# Bathtime

First Aladdin Books edition 1990
Text copyright © 1983, 1988 by Walker Books Ltd
Illustrations copyright © 1988 by Maureen Roffey

Aladdin Books
Macmillan Publishing Company
866 Third Avenue, New York, NY 10022
Printed in Hong Kong

A hardcover edition of *Bathtime* is available from
Four Winds Press, Macmillan Publishing Company.
10   9   8   7   6   5   4   3   2   1

Library of Congress Cataloging-in-Publication Data

Roffey, Maureen.
Bathtime/Maureen Roffey. — 1st Aladdin Books ed. p.      cm.
Summary: Two youngsters who have gotten dirty playing prepare
for their bath, enjoy the adventure of getting clean again,
and finish their other preparations for bedtime.
ISBN 0-689-70808-4
[1. Baths—Fiction.] I. Title. [PZ7.R6255Bat      1990] [E]—dc20
89-18413 CIP AC

# Bathtime

## Maureen Roffey

Aladdin Books
Macmillan Publishing Company
New York

There are so many ways
to get in a mess!

How do you get in a mess?

It's bathtime.
The faucets are on.

Water splashes. Water is wet.
What else can you say about water?

# Time to get into the bathtub.

# Which clothes do you take off first?

Which clothes do you take off last?

Bathtime is good for playing. Which toys do you play with at bathtime?

# Lots of things belong to bathtime. How many of these do you have?

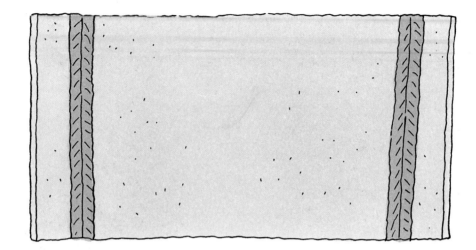

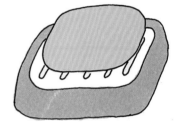

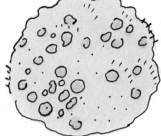

Baths are for washing all over.

# Which parts do you wash at bathtime?

# Bathtime is over. Pull the plug.

# Where does all the water go?

# Rub-a-dub-dub. It's drying time.

You dry your face . . . your arms . . .

your legs . . . your back.

What else do you dry?

# What clothes do you put on after bathtime?

# Don't forget your teeth . . .

# and hair.

Now pop into bed.

Story time.
What is your favorite story?

Snuggle down.

# Good night. Sleep tight.